HIP HOP

Carmel Reilly

NELSON
CENGAGE Learning™

Australia • Brazil • Japan • Korea • Mexico • Singapore • Spain • United Kingdom • United States

Hip Hop

Fast Forward
Green Level 13

Text: Carmel Reilly
Editor: Johanna Rohan
Design: James Lowe
Series design: James Lowe
Production controller: Emma Hayes
Photo research: Michelle Cottrill
Audio recordings: Juliet Hill, Picture Start
Spoken by: Matthew King and Abbe Holmes
Reprint: Jennifer Foo

Acknowledgements
The author and publisher would like to acknowledge
permission to reproduce material from the following sources:
Photographs by Alamy/Stockbyte, p18 left; Australian Picture
Library/Corbis Saba/Marc Asnin/Corbis/Jacques M Chenet,
p10/ Lynn Goldsmith, pp 12, 13/ Zefa/ H Sitton, p 23 left; Getty
Images, p20/ Bruno Vincent, p21/ Dave M Bennet, p5 bottom/
Frank Micelotta, front cover, pp 1, 9 bottom/ Frederick M
Brown, p4 top/ Hulton Archive, p 7/ Ray Tamarra, p9 top/
Reportage, p 4 bottom/ Scott Gries, pp 8, 19 right/ Stone+ p19
left/ Taxi, pp 3, 22, 23 right; Image 100, back cover;
Photolibrary.com/ Martha Cooper, p16-17/ Alamy/ Joe Sohm,
p6/ Suzy Bennet, p14/ Superstock, p11 bottom; Thomson
Learning Australia/ Michelle Cottrill, p5 top, 18 right.

Text © 2007 Cengage Learning Australia Pty Limited
Illustrations © 2007 Cengage Learning Australia Pty Limited

ISBN 978 0 17 012580 2
ISBN 978 0 17 012573 4 (set)

Cengage Learning Australia
Level 7, 80 Dorcas Street
South Melbourne, Victoria Australia 3205
Phone: 1300 790 853

Cengage Learning New Zealand
Unit 4B Rosedale Office Park
331 Rosedale Road, Albany, North Shore NZ 0632
Phone: 0800 449 725

For learning solutions, visit **cengage.com.au**

Printed in Australia by Ligare Pty Ltd
7 8 9 10 11 12 13 21 20 19 18 17

THE UNIVERSITY OF
MELBOURNE

Evaluated in independent research by staff from the
Department of Language, Literacy and Arts Education
at the University of Melbourne.

Carmel Reilly

Contents

Chapter 1	**Hip Hop**	4
Chapter 2	**In the Bronx**	6
Chapter 3	**Rap Music**	8
Chapter 4	**Break Dancing**	12
Chapter 5	**Graffiti Art**	16
Chapter 6	**Hip Hop Today**	20
Glossary and Index		24

HIP HOP

When most people think of hip hop, they think of:

- rap music

- break dancing

• graffiti art

• DJing.

But, hip hop is also a **culture**.
It has its own way of talking, dressing
and thinking about things.

IN THE BRONX

Hip hop started in the Bronx in New York in the 1970s.
The Bronx is an African-American neighbourhood.

the Bronx

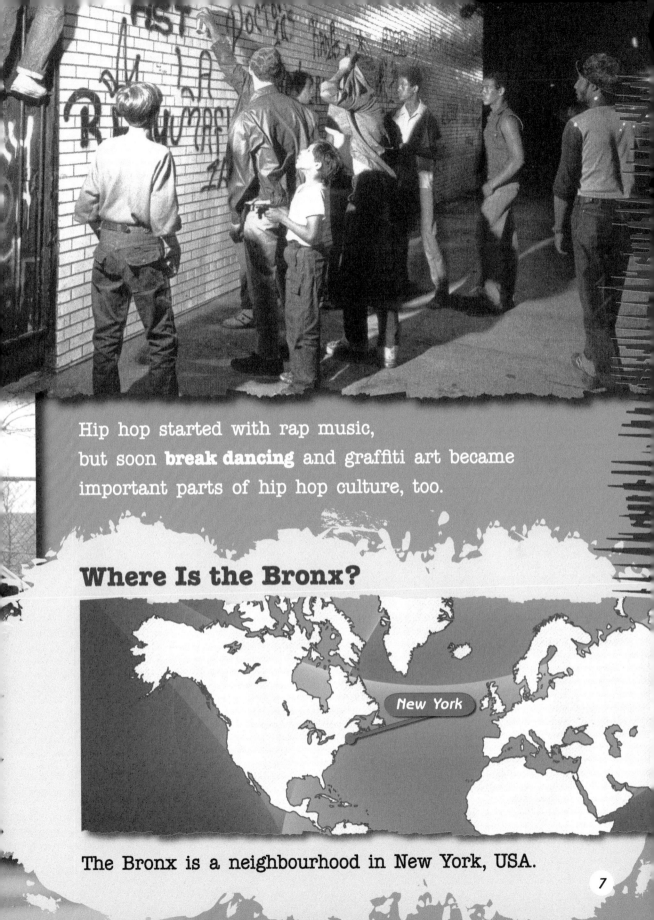

Hip hop started with rap music, but soon **break dancing** and graffiti art became important parts of hip hop culture, too.

Where Is the Bronx?

New York

The Bronx is a neighbourhood in New York, USA.

Chapter 3

RAP MUSIC

In the 1970s, DJs from Jamaica started playing at parties in the Bronx.

These DJs had different ways of playing records from other DJs.

They liked to play parts of a song, and then say things in between.

Jamaican DJ Kool Herc was one of the first hip hop DJs.

DJ Clark Kent

The music in the song was called the **break**.
The spoken part was called **rapping**.

DJ Grandmaster Flash

As rap music started to take off,
DJs started to use rapping to talk about
all kinds of things.

Big Daddy Kane

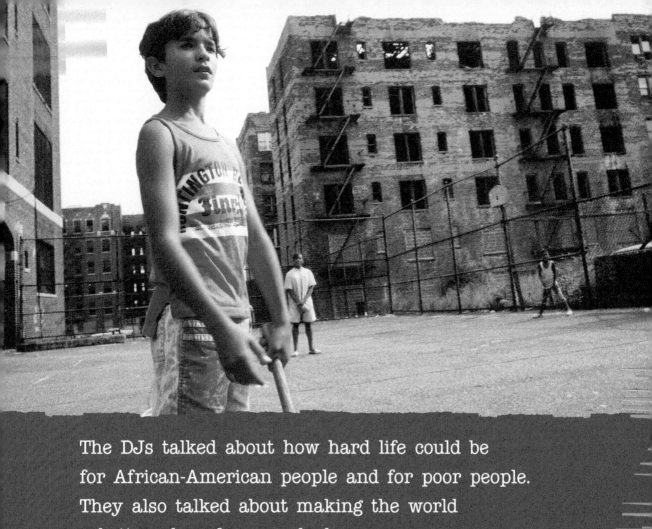

The DJs talked about how hard life could be
for African-American people and for poor people.
They also talked about making the world
a better place for everybody.

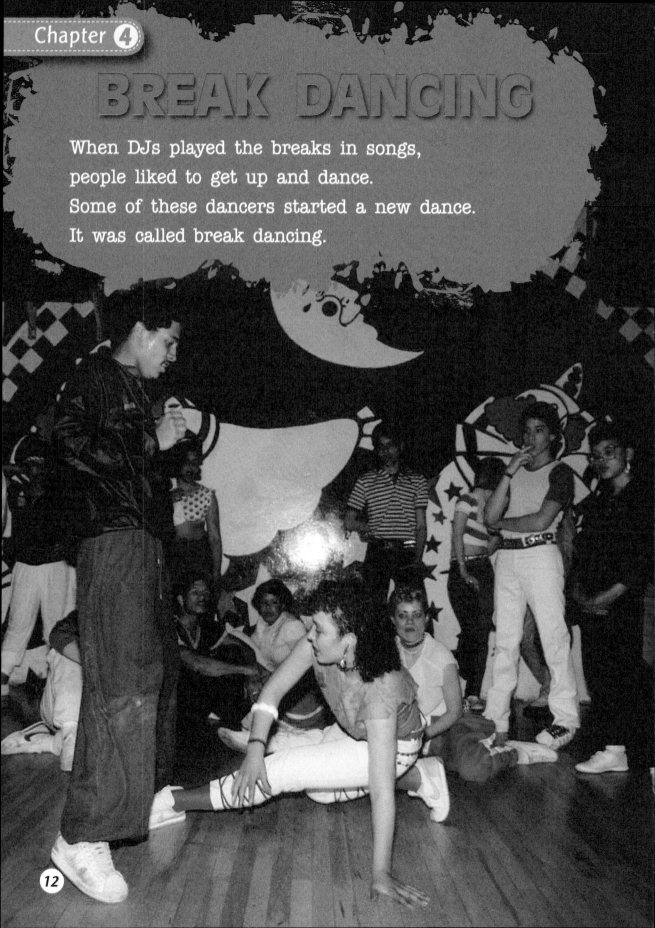

Chapter 4

BREAK DANCING

When DJs played the breaks in songs,
people liked to get up and dance.
Some of these dancers started a new dance.
It was called break dancing.

Break dancing was very different from
any other kind of dancing.
Break dancers had to do
a lot of very hard moves.

Break dancers took this new dance
into other neighbourhoods.
They set up a music player
and danced on the street.
People loved to look at them
and gave them money.

Break dancing became very big
in many places around the world.

Chapter 5

GRAFFITI ART

Graffiti art is an important part
of hip hop culture, too.

Painting on public spaces isn't legal.
But, some people liked graffiti art a lot.
They asked city councils to make it legal
in some places.
The councils said yes, and handed over
some public spaces
for artists to paint on!

People liked graffiti art so much
that they started to use it on other things —
like on clothes and record covers.

Graffiti art is a big part of hip hop today.

Chapter 6

HIP HOP TODAY

It took a long time for hip hop to become popular outside African-American neighbourhoods.

Eminem

Missy Elliot performing in Edinburgh, Scotland

Today DJing, rap music, break dancing and graffiti art are popular all around the world.

But, for people in places like the Bronx,
hip hop is about more than just
the music and the art.

It's a way for these people to talk to each other and tell the world about their lives, their culture and their ideas.

Glossary

break — the music in a hip hop song where no words are spoken

break dancing — an energetic style of street dancing started by African-Americans in New York in the 1970s

culture — the behaviour and traditions of a group of people

rapping — when the words to a song are spoken rapidly over the music

Index

Big Daddy Kane 10
break dancing 4, 7, 12–15, 21
the Bronx 6–7, 8, 22

DJ Clark Kent 9
DJ Grandmaster Flash 9
DJ Kool Herc 8

Eminem 20

graffiti art 5, 7, 16–19, 21

Missy Elliot 21

rap music 4, 7, 8–11, 21

Ice on Earth

Nicolas Brasch

NELSON
CENGAGE Learning·

Australia • Brazil • Japan • Korea • Mexico • Singapore • Spain • United Kingdom • United States

NELSON
CENGAGE Learning

Ice on Earth

Fast Forward
Yellow Level 7

Text: Nicolas Brasch
Illustrations: Boris Silvestri
Editor: Kate McGough
Designer: James Lowe
Series Design: James Lowe
Production Controller: Emma Hayes
Photo Research: Michelle Cottrill

Acknowledgements
The author and publisher would like to acknowledge
permission to reproduce material from the following sources:
Photographs by Masterfile/ Dale Wilson, p. 13/ Daryl Benson,
pp. 14-15; National Science Foundation/ Jeffery Kietzmann,
back cover, front cover, pp. 1, 3; NOAA/ Michael Van Woert, p.
12; Photolibrary.com/ Alan Kearney, p. 5/ Ben Osbourne, pp. 6
-7/ Benelux Press, pp. 10-11/ Doug Alan, pp. 8-9; Photos.com,
p. 4.

ISBN 978 0 17 012508 6
ISBN 978 0 17 012511 6 (set)

Cengage Learning Australia
Level 7, 80 Dorcas Street
South Melbourne, Victoria Australia 3205
Phone: 1300 790 853

Cengage Learning New Zealand
Unit 4B Rosedale Office Park
331 Rosedale Road, Albany, North Shore NZ 0632
Phone: 0800 449 725

For learning solutions, visit **cengage.com.au**

Printed in Australia by Ligare Pty Ltd
7 8 9 10 11 12 13 20 19 18 17 16

THE UNIVERSITY OF
MELBOURNE

Evaluated in independent research by staff from the
Department of Language, Literacy and Arts Education
at the University of Melbourne.